My dearest puppy, Storm,

I hope this letter reaches you safe and sound. You have been so brave since you had to flee from the evil wolf Shadow.

Do not worry about me. I will hide here until you are strong enough to return and lead our pack. For now you must move on – you must hide from Shadow and his spies. If Shadow finds this letter I believe he will try to destroy it . . .

Find a good friend – someone to help finish my message to you. Because what I have to say to you is important. What I have to say is this: you must always

Please don't feel lonely. Trust in your friends and all will be well.

Your loving mother,

Canista

Sue Bentley's books for children often include animals, fairies and wildlife. She lives in Northampton and enjoys reading, going to the cinema, relaxing by her garden pond and watching the birds feeding their babies on the lawn. At school she was always getting told off for daydreaming or staring out of the window – but she now realizes that she was storing up ideas for when she became a writer. She has met and owned many cats and dogs and each one has brought a special kind of magic to her life.

Sue Bentley

Magic Puppy

Classroom Princess

Illustrated by Angela Swan

PUFFIN

To Pash – gorgeous, charming spotty girl . . .
except for the snail-crunching!

PUFFIN BOOKS

Published by the Penguin Group
Penguin Books Ltd, 80 Strand, London WC2R 0RL, England
Penguin Group (USA) Inc., 375 Hudson Street, New York, New York 10014, USA
Penguin Group (Canada), 90 Eglinton Avenue East, Suite 700, Toronto, Ontario, Canada M4P 2Y3
(a division of Pearson Penguin Canada Inc.)
Penguin Ireland, 25 St Stephen's Green, Dublin 2, Ireland (a division of Penguin Books Ltd)
Penguin Group (Australia), 250 Camberwell Road, Camberwell, Victoria 3124, Australia
(a division of Pearson Australia Group Pty Ltd)
Penguin Books India Pvt Ltd, 11 Community Centre, Panchsheel Park, New Delhi – 110 017, India
Penguin Group (NZ), 67 Apollo Drive, Rosedale, North Shore 0632, New Zealand
(a division of Pearson New Zealand Ltd)
Penguin Books (South Africa) (Pty) Ltd, 24 Sturdee Avenue, Rosebank,
Johannesburg 2196, South Africa

Penguin Books Ltd, Registered Offices: 80 Strand, London WC2R 0RL, England

puffinbooks.com

First published 2009
1

Text copyright © Sue Bentley, 2009
Illustrations copyright © Angela Swan, 2009
All rights reserved

The moral right of the author and illustrator has been asserted

Set in Bembo
Made and printed in England by Clays Ltd, St Ives plc

British Library Cataloguing in Publication Data
A CIP catalogue record for this book is available from the British Library

ISBN: 978–0–141–32479–1

Mixed Sources
Product group from well-managed
forests and other controlled sources
www.fsc.org Cert no. SA-COC-1592
© 1996 Forest Stewardship Council

Penguin Books is committed to a sustainable future
for our business, our readers and our planet.
The book in your hands is made from paper
certified by the Forest Stewardship Council.

Prologue

Storm glanced up at the snow clouds gathering over the dark mountain slopes. It felt good to be back in his home world.

Suddenly, the young silver-grey wolf stiffened as a terrifying howl echoed on the still air.

'Shadow!' Storm gasped. The fierce lone wolf who had attacked the Moon-claw pack was very close.

He should have known that it was not safe to return. He needed to find a place to hide, and quickly.

There was a dazzling flash of bright light and a shower of gold sparks. Where the young wolf had been standing there now crouched a tiny fluffy brown-and-white King Charles spaniel puppy with bright midnight-blue eyes and a silky tail.

Storm hoped this disguise would protect him until he was under cover.

The tiny puppy's heart beat fast as he leapt forward and bounded up a steep slope. Storm looked from right to left as he ran, his little floppy ears flying out behind him, but there was nowhere to hide. No scrubby trees or bushes, not even a clump of grass.

As Storm felt himself tiring, he spotted

a cluster of rocks. Perhaps there would be a small space he could squeeze into. But as the dark shape of a large wolf came into view, the tiny puppy whimpered with alarm.

This was it. Shadow had found him!

'This way, my son!' called the wolf in a deep velvety growl. 'There is a cave where we will be safe for a while.'

'Mother!' Storm woofed in relief. He scrambled over the rocks and followed Canista as she led him down into the cave.

As the darkness closed over Storm, he licked his mother's muzzle in greeting, wriggling all over and wagging his tail.

Canista reached out a huge grey paw that was bigger than Storm was now and scooped her disguised cub against her warm furry side.

'I am glad to see you again, but you have returned at a dangerous time. Shadow is hunting for you. He wants to lead the Moon-claw pack, but the others will not follow him. They will wait until you are strong enough to become leader.'

Storm's bright blue eyes flared with anger and sorrow. 'Is it not enough that Shadow has killed my father and all my litter brothers and wounded you? Let us fight him and force him to leave our land!'

Canista's face softened as she gazed at her brave little cub. 'I am still too weak from Shadow's poisonous bite and you cannot face him alone. Use this disguise. Go back to the other world and return when you are stronger.'

As she finished speaking, Storm saw
her face cloud with pain. He leaned
forward and huffed out a warm puppy
breath filled with a thousand tiny gold
stars. The sparkling mist swirled round
Canista's sore leg for a moment and then
sank into her fur and disappeared.

'Thank you. The pain is lessening,' she
growled softly.

Suddenly, there came the sound of
mighty paws digging at the rocks outside.
An enormous wolf's head was outlined
against the sky at the cave's entrance.

'Go, Storm! Save yourself!' Canista urged.

Storm whimpered as bright gold sparks
ignited in his fluffy brown-and-white fur
and he felt the power building inside him.
A bright golden glow grew around him.
And grew brighter still . . .

Chapter
ONE

Kelsey Fisher frowned as she saw a car
pull up outside. The doors sprang open
and her dad's new girlfriend, Jo Wright,
and her twin daughters got out.

'What are *they* doing here so early?'
Kelsey wondered.

It was Saturday morning and she was still
in her pyjamas. They had been a Christmas
present from her mum, who now lived

in Australia with her new husband and
Kelsey's little half-brother. The pyjamas
had a pattern of little blue teddies and
pink bows and Kelsey adored them, even
though they were much too small for her.

As footsteps came thundering up the
stairs, Kelsey quickly leapt back into bed
and dived under the duvet to hide her
pyjamas from the older girls.

The bedroom door banged open and
Anna and Louise exploded into her room.

'Surprise!' Anna said cheerfully. 'Mum's
taking us all to the new riding stables.'

'You're coming too! There's probably a
quiet pony you can ride,' Louise added.

Kelsey couldn't think of anything worse.
Ponies terrified her. There was no way
she was going anywhere near one. But if
the twins found out that she was scared
of ponies, they'd tease her even more than
they usually did. 'Thanks . . . but I'm . . . er
. . . having a lie-in,' she said quickly.

'That's what you think!' Anna grabbed
Kelsey's pillow and started bashing her
with it. *Whump! Whump!*

'Give that back!' Kelsey cried, leaping
up and making a lunge for her pillow.

'What soppy PJs. They don't even fit

you!' Louise said, giggling.

Kelsey blushed hotly. She grappled with Anna, but Anna was bigger than she was and much stronger. Anna threw the pillow to Louise, who caught it and tossed it on to the floor and then both of them pulled Kelsey's duvet off.

'Now you *have* to get up!' Anna crowed.

Kelsey's dad appeared in the bedroom doorway. 'What's all this hoo-ha about? Ah, a pillow fight! Having fun?' he said, smiling.

It's not fun, when it's one-sided, Kelsey thought bitterly. *Or should that be two-sided, if it involved twins?*

'We're trying to persuade Kelsey to come out with us. But she doesn't want to,' Louise cried.

Her dad frowned. 'Why's that, Kelsey?'

Kelsey scrunched herself up against the
back of her bed and folded her arms tightly
across her chest. 'I can't go, because . . . I've
got . . . um . . . tummy ache. I must have
eaten too much pizza last night,' she said.

Jo peered over Kelsey's dad's shoulder.
'Why's everyone in here?' she asked,

puzzled. Jo had a friendly smile and gentle blue eyes.

'Kelsey's not coming with us, Mum. She got pizza blow-out!' Anna said.

'Poor old you.' Jo's pretty face creased in concern as she looked at Kelsey. 'Would you like to just come and watch? You might feel better in the fresh air.'

Kelsey stared at the floor. 'I'd rather just stay here with Dad,' she said quietly.

'Maybe that would be best. It's a shame you're sick, but you can always come riding another time,' Jo said kindly. 'Come on, you two. We'd best be off. I hope you feel better soon, Kelsey. See you later.'

The twins followed their mum out. 'See ya! Wouldn't wanna be ya!' they chorused from the doorway.

Kelsey tingled with embarrassment as

she heard them giggling all the way down the stairs. Her dad went down to the front door to see them out and the house was suddenly quiet.

Kelsey sighed. She wasn't sure how she felt about her dad having a girlfriend. It had been fine for the last couple of years with just the two of them. Jo seemed quite nice and she might even get to like her, but the twins were so hyper and full of themselves. Kelsey didn't even know if she wanted to make friends with them.

Mr Fisher came back into the room as Kelsey was straightening the bedclothes.

'Those twins are real live-wires, aren't they? You'll have to start sticking up for yourself a bit more around them, love,' he commented.

Kelsey nodded, blinking hard so he

wouldn't notice her wet eyes. That was easy for *him* to say.

'Will you be OK by yourself for a while, if I get on with some work?' he asked, ruffling her curly light-brown hair. Her dad designed and built websites and sometimes worked from home.

Kelsey managed a wobbly smile. 'I've stopped feeling sick now. I think I'll go

and read in the old summer house to
cheer myself up.'

'Good idea. You love it down there.
Don't forget to wrap up well. It's quite
mild today, but it's still only January.'

'I will,' she told him.

'Right you are. Give me a shout if you
need anything.'

As soon as he'd gone, Kelsey leapt out
of bed and threw on her clothes. Grabbing
her favourite book of dog stories and a
fleece blanket, she went outside and down
to the bottom of the garden. The summer
house was a small wooden building
nestling among the trees. She had played
there with her dolls when she was little
and a lot of her old toys were stored there.

Kelsey found a garden chair and
snuggled up inside her blanket to read.

The stories were so thrilling that she didn't notice time passing. One hour and then another ticked by. She was in the middle of a really exciting story about a lost puppy when, suddenly, a dazzling flash of bright gold light lit up the entire summer house.

'Oh!' Kelsey almost jumped out of her skin. It must have been lightning. She looked up from her book, expecting to hear a roll of thunder at any moment.

To her amazement, right in front of her was a tiny fluffy brown-and-white puppy. It looked up at her with enormous midnight-blue eyes.

'Please help me,' it woofed.

Chapter
TWO

Kelsey did a double take. The book slipped off her lap and landed on the floor with a *thud*. She must have been so engrossed in her story that she'd just imagined the tiny puppy had spoken to her!

There was a big fence all round the garden and Kelsey couldn't see how a tiny puppy had climbed over it. Shrugging off the blanket, she got out of the chair and

looked down at the tiny puppy in front
of her. 'Hello there. Where did you come
from?'

The puppy put its head on one side.
'I used my magic to come to this world. I
need to hide from my enemies. My name
is Storm of the Moon-claw pack. What is
yours?' it woofed politely.

'Oh!' Kelsey gasped, taking a step back.
As the backs of her knees brushed her chair,

she sat down again with a jolt. 'You . . . you really can . . . sp-speak!' she stammered.

The puppy nodded. He sat down and curled his silky tail round his little brown-and-white body. Despite his tiny size Storm didn't seem to be afraid of her. He was looking at Kelsey curiously and seemed to be waiting for her to reply.

'I'm . . . um . . . Kelsey. Kelsey Fisher,' she said. 'I live here in Long Morton with my dad.'

Storm dipped his tiny head in a formal bow. 'I am honoured to meet you, Kelsey.'

'Um . . . me too,' Kelsey said.

She was still having trouble taking all this in, but she didn't want to frighten this amazing little puppy away. Kelsey slowly got up again and then crouched down to make herself seem smaller and less threatening.

'Why do you need to hide? Is someone after you?' she asked softly.

Storm's unusual blue eyes darkened as he nodded. 'A fierce lone wolf attacked my Moon-claw pack. He is called Shadow. Shadow killed my father and litter brothers and wounded my mother. He wants to be leader, but the other wolves want to wait until I can lead them.'

Kelsey blinked at him in surprise. 'But how can you lead a wolf pack? You're just a tiny pup–'

'Keep back, please!' Storm ordered.

Before Kelsey knew what was happening, there was another brilliant flash of light and a fountain of gold sparks gushed out all around her, before drifting harmlessly to the summer-house floor.

The tiny brown-and-white puppy had

disappeared and in its place a regal-looking young silver-grey wolf stood there proudly, almost filling the summer house. Its thick neck-ruff glimmered with thousands of tiny lights like gold gems.

'Storm?' Kelsey asked anxiously, eyeing the young wolf's sharp teeth, enormous paws and muscular body.

'Yes, Kelsey, it is me. Do not be afraid. I will not harm you,' Storm said in a deep velvety growl.

Before Kelsey had time to get used to Storm in this majestic form, there was a final dazzling bright flash of gold light and Storm reappeared as a tiny fluffy brown-and-white puppy with huge midnight-blue eyes.

'Oh! That was incredible!' Kelsey breathed. 'What a brilliant disguise.'

'Yes, but Shadow will see through it, if he finds me,' Storm yapped softly. 'I am in danger. I need to hide now.'

Kelsey saw that the tiny puppy had tucked his tail between his back legs and was beginning to tremble all over. Her heart went out to him. Storm was stunning as his real wolf-self, but as a small ball of soft brown-and-white fur he was totally adorable.

Kelsey held out her hand and rubbed the

tips of her fingers together encouragingly.
Storm edged closer until his little wet
brown nose brushed her fingers. Kelsey
picked him up and Storm licked her chin
with his pink tongue.

Smiling, Kelsey stroked his soft little
head. 'What am I going to do with you?
You'll be lonely hiding in the summer
house, all by yourself. I'll ask Dad if I can
keep you. He'll understand. He knows
that I've always wanted a puppy to be my
special friend and sleep in my bedroom.'

Storm showed his sharp little teeth in a
doggy grin. 'I would like that very much.'

'Let's go into the office and ask him
now. I can't wait to tell Dad all about you –'
Kelsey broke off as Storm reared up and
placed one tiny brown-and-white front
paw on her cheek.

'No! You can tell no one my secret. You must promise me, Kelsey,' he yapped, his little heart-shaped face suddenly serious.

Kelsey felt a bit disappointed that she couldn't share her brilliant news with her dad. He would have loved to know about Storm. It would have to be a really special secret all of her own — one that not even the twins knew about.

'OK. I promise. Cross my heart. No one's going to hear about you from me,' she said.

Storm's muzzle lifted in a grin. 'Thank you, Kelsey.'

As Kelsey stepped out of the summer house with Storm in her arms, she saw Anna and Louise striding down the lawn towards her. They looked hot and red-faced and their boots and jeans were muddy.

'You just missed a brilliant riding lesson –'
Anna began and then her eyes widened as
she spotted Storm. 'Wow! Where did that
cute puppy come from?'

'Did your dad buy it for us all to share?
Give it me. I want to hold it!' Louise
ordered, holding out her arms.

Kelsey stood there uncertainly, feeling
tongue-tied by her usual shyness. But
then a surge of protectiveness for Storm

swept over her. 'Storm's a "he" not an "it",' she found herself blurting out, to her own surprise. 'I'd better keep hold of him for now. He's quite nervous until he gets used to you.'

Louise and Anna exchanged amazed glances. Kelsey marched past them while they were silent for once.

Chapter
THREE

'I don't know, Kelsey, you know how I feel about kids having pets,' Mr Fisher said ten minutes later when Kelsey had finished giving her version of how she had found Storm in the summer house. 'They have a habit of getting bored with them in no time and then the poor old parents are the ones who have to look after them. I think we'll phone the RSPCA. They'll find him a good home.'

Kelsey and Storm stood in the small kitchen, next to Jo and the twins. 'But I won't get bored with Storm! He's special, Dad! He chose me to look after him,' Kelsey exclaimed. *Oh no, she hadn't meant to say that! She must be more careful.*

Luckily her dad just laughed. 'You and your imagination, Kelsey Fisher!'

Kelsey bit her lip, feeling her colour rise. How could she change her dad's mind? He just *had* to let Storm live with them. Storm was in danger and only she could keep him safe.

'Please, Dad,' she rushed on. 'I promise that I'll look after him. He can sleep in my room and I'll buy his food from my pocket money and everything.'

Mr Fisher looked surprised. 'Well, I

haven't seen you this passionate about
something for a long while! You're usually
such a quiet little mouse. Is this really
important to you?'

'D-Definitely,' Kelsey gulped.

'Storm looks like a little King Charles
spaniel,' Jo commented. She turned
to Kelsey's dad. 'Maybe it would be a
good idea for Kelsey to look after him,
at least until an owner turns up. Being
responsible for a pet can do a lot for a
person's self-confidence,' she said.

Mr Fisher wavered. 'That's true,' he said, looking at Kelsey thoughtfully.

Kelsey didn't even mind that they were talking about her as if she wasn't standing right there. 'So, can I keep him then, Dad?' she asked, crossing her fingers and all her toes. 'Storm can sleep in my bedroom and –'

'That's not fair! Storm should live at our house sometimes if we're going to share him,' Louise grumbled.

'Yeah. He's going to be our dog too, isn't he? I'm going to get him a collar and a dog chew from the pet shop,' Anna cried.

'But he's not your . . .' Kelsey's shoulders sagged and her voice tailed away. The twins were impossible when they were in full-on bossy mode. She wished she could just point the TV remote at them and press the Pause button.

Jo stepped forward. 'Hold your horses, you two!' she snapped at the twins. 'Who said anything about puppy-sharing? Storm belongs to Kelsey. She found him in her garden. So he's her responsibility. I'm sure she'll ask us for help if she needs it. Isn't that right, Kelsey?'

Kelsey nodded.

'Aw, Mum!' the twins complained.

'That's enough! I'm not going to argue with you,' Jo said in a warning tone.

The twins got the message.

Kelsey was too amazed to speak. She had never expected Jo to be on *her* side.

Her dad smiled in his usual easy-going way. 'Well, it looks as if that's settled. You can keep Storm, Kelsey. But if an owner turns up, there'll be no arguments. Understood?'

Kelsey nodded happily. She knew that no one was going to come and claim this particular puppy! 'Thanks, Dad. I'm just going to take Storm upstairs to make him a bed and then I'll go to the shops to buy him some food.' She beamed gratefully at Jo on her way out. 'Um . . . Thanks,' she said quietly.

Jo smiled back, her blue eyes twinkling.

She squeezed Kelsey's shoulder gently. 'You're welcome!'

Halfway up the stairs, Kelsey paused with Storm in her arms, half expecting Anna and Louise to come haring after her and insist on 'helping' her with Storm. But no one followed her. It actually seemed quiet and calm downstairs.

In her bedroom, Kelsey kissed the top of Storm's fluffy little head and then placed him on her bed, where he turned round in circles before making himself comfortable.

'I like it here. This is a safe place,' Storm yawned.

Kelsey smiled at him. She felt a warm glow of happiness as she realized that she now had a special magical friend — a secret just for herself.

*

'Are you going to be OK while I'm at school today?' Kelsey asked Storm after breakfast on Monday morning.

Storm was curled up on her lap under the table. 'I will come with you. I like school,' he woofed.

Kelsey looked down at him in amazement. Storm knew about school! He was full of surprises.

'Well, OK, then,' she said, still not quite sure about having a puppy in her class all day, 'but I'll have to hide you inside my school bag, in case Miss Armitage notices you. She's my class teacher.'

Storm's big midnight-blue eyes looked at her with eagerness. 'Do not worry. I will use my magic so that only you can see and hear me.'

'You can make yourself invisible? Cool! There's no problem, then!' Kelsey said delightedly. 'Maybe you should do it now in case Dad sees you leaving with me.'

Kelsey felt a slight tingling sensation down her spine. Little gold sparks bloomed in Storm's silky brown-and-white fur and then faded immediately.

'It is done,' Storm woofed.

Chapter
FOUR

Kelsey walked to school with Storm
trotting along invisibly beside her. She
still expected someone to notice her new
puppy and ask about him. But when no
one did, she slowly began to relax, smiling
at the thought of her very special secret.

As Kelsey and Storm walked through
the school gates, Kelsey spotted Anna and
Louise. The twins were in the year above

her and were standing chatting with a group of older girls.

'Hiya, Kelsey,' Anna shouted, waving eagerly.

'Hey! How's that mega-gorgeous little puppy?' boomed Louise.

Kelsey hid a smile as she thought how amazed they would be if they knew that Storm was right under their noses, but of course they couldn't see him! 'Storm's fine, thanks,' she answered.

'We're coming over to your house with Mum after school tomorrow. And Louise and me are going to take Storm for a walk just to help you out,' Anna said enthusiastically.

'That's OK. I'm doing fine with him, thanks,' Kelsey said, determined not to let the twins take up all of Storm's time.

Anna didn't reply and Kelsey was
surprised to see that she actually looked
crestfallen at this.

'Haven't you ever heard that sharing is
caring?' one of the girls from the twins'

group called out. Kelsey's heart began thumping as the whole group of older girls all turned to look at her.

Kelsey ignored them and luckily the next moment the bell went and she turned quickly towards the safety of her classroom.

Surprised by Kelsey's sudden movement, Storm scampered forward, almost tripping her up. Kelsey did a hasty sidestep, to avoid treading on the little puppy and barged straight into a boy from her class.

'Oof!' It was Ross Kirk, a fairly new boy who had only lived in Long Morton for a few months. There was a *thud* as the pile of books Ross was carrying crashed to the ground.

The twins and their friends all giggled. Kelsey went hot. She hated how she blushed all the time.

'Watch out!' Ross said crossly, going redder than Kelsey. Even his ears glowed.

'Sorry, Ross,' Kelsey murmured. She bent down to pick up one of the books, but some loose pages fluttered out and were whipped across the playground by a stiff breeze. 'I'll get them!' she called.

As Kelsey ran about chasing pages, Storm scampered around helpfully snapping pages out of the air and jumping on others, so that Kelsey could gather them all up.

'Thanks, Storm,' Kelsey whispered as she returned with the book to Ross. 'Um . . . sorry. Some of the pages got a bit messed up.'

'I can see that!' Ross complained, looking confused at what Kelsey realized were puppy teethmarks! 'This is a school

library book. You know how Miss
Armitage's always going on about how
we're supposed to look after them. I'll
probably get double detention.'

Kelsey felt really bad for him. She
wanted to help, but didn't know what she
could do.

But Storm did. He jumped up, pawing
at her skirt to get her attention. 'Ask Ross
to give the book to you!' he woofed.

Kelsey wasn't sure what Storm was
planning, but she already trusted him. She
didn't hesitate. 'Give me the book, Ross.
I'll . . . um . . . try and fix it.'

Ross frowned suspiciously, but he handed
it over. 'OK, then. But if Miss Armitage
asks me where it is, I'm telling her you've
got it. I'm not doing detention for you as
well as me!' Thrusting his hands into his

pockets, he went into school.

All the other kids had gone inside now, including Anna, Louise and their friends.

Kelsey stood in the empty playground with Storm.

'Crikey! Ross's moody, isn't he? Anyone would think I dropped his book on purpose,' she said, looking down at Storm. 'Why did you want him to give it to me anyway?'

Storm's little muzzle creased in a mysterious smile and Kelsey felt another warm prickling sensation flow down her spine. But it was much stronger this time.

Glittering sparks glowed in Storm's brown-and-white fur and his little floppy ears crackled with electricity. Lifting a front paw, he sent a glittering jet of sparks whooshing towards the battered library book in Kelsey's hands.

She watched in complete amazement as the book fanned open by itself. A swarm

of sparkles like tiny fireflies whizzed
between the pages. They busily rubbed
out muddy marks, smoothed out creases
and teethmarks and stuck all the loose
pages back in place.

In no time at all, the book was as good
as new. Then it closed with a loud *snap!*
and Kelsey saw that every last golden
spark had faded from Storm's silky fur.

'That's fantastic. It's as good as new.
Thanks, Storm!'

'You are welcome,' he woofed.

Kelsey grinned at him, wondering what
else her marvellous little friend could do.

Storm sat on Kelsey's lap while Miss
Armitage took the register, but he soon
jumped down and went exploring.

Kelsey smiled as she saw him snuffling

around the school bag of one of her
classmates. She thought that he could
probably smell the girl's pet dog or cat.

'Now, class. Pay attention,' Miss Armitage
said. She had lovely curly dark-red hair,
which she wore in a pony tail. 'As you
know we've been looking at festivals, such
as Diwali, Easter and Rosh Hashanah
this term. And this weekend we'll be
celebrating our local Wassail night festival
here in Long Morton. Now, I've got some
very exciting news for you. This year's
Wassail Apple Prince and Princess will be
chosen from *this* class.'

Some of the class started cheering and
clapping.

'Yay! I hope it's me, Miss!' said Mandy,
a girl with long dark hair and olive skin.

Kelsey hoped it would be Mandy too.

She didn't fancy wearing a crown and cloak
and leading the procession through the old
orchard in front of hundreds of people.

From the corner of her eye, Kelsey
noticed Storm ambling back towards
her. He jumped on to her lap and then
climbed up on to her desk. As he sat
down, his silky tail swept against her
pencil case and she just caught it before it
was knocked to the floor.

Kelsey gasped inwardly, but luckily
everyone was listening to the teacher and
no one noticed.

'I am sorry,' Storm yapped.

'Doesn't matter. No one saw. Did
you have a good mooch about?' Kelsey
whispered, smiling.

Storm nodded. 'Yes. There are lots of
exciting smells in here,' he panted happily,

his pink tongue hanging out.

'Pay attention, please, Kelsey. Who can tell me what wassail means?' Miss Armitage's voice rang out.

'Good health,' a boy called Simon cried.

'Simon's right. It's from the Anglo-Saxon "*wes hal*". Does anyone know how long the wassail tradition goes back?' Miss Armitage looked pointedly at Kelsey.

Kelsey pretended that she hadn't noticed and slipped down in her seat.

'Kelsey, do sit up straight!' the teacher said briskly. 'Answer the question, now. Speak up, dear.'

'Um . . . does it go back hundreds of years?' Kelsey guessed, willing herself not to blush.

Miss Armitage nodded her approval.

'Kelsey's right. Although no one knows for sure. Wassail was probably invented by farmers who were tired and worn out after the Christmas merrymaking. They knew they had hard winter work to look forward to and they needed something to pick them up.'

'My gran has a pick-me-up every night in her cocoa,' Simon said cheekily.

Miss Armitage gave him one of her looks. A lot of kids laughed.

Despite herself, Kelsey couldn't help smiling. She noticed that Ross wasn't laughing. He sat by himself, looking pale and tense.

'Get your workbooks out, please. You can start on your designs for musical instruments and lanterns,' Miss Armitage said.

Kelsey began working on a drawing for her lantern. While everyone was occupied, the teacher scribbled down everyone's name from the register on scraps of paper and put them into a small bag.

Kelsey looked up from her drawing for a moment and saw that Ross still wore the same tense expression. He hadn't drawn very much, either. 'I wonder if he's still worried about getting into trouble because of his library book,' she whispered to Storm.

She didn't think she could risk nipping across to Ross's desk with the book. Miss Armitage was bound to notice and ask awkward questions. She'd have to give it to him later.

Storm craned his little neck to look at Ross. 'He seems like a very quiet boy.'

Kelsey nodded. 'He never speaks to many people in class and I don't think he's made many friends. He must be quite lonely.'

Storm's furry little brow wrinkled in a frown.

Kelsey had just turned back to the lantern design when she suddenly felt a familiar warm tingling sensation down her backbone. She gave a small gasp as bright gold sparks ignited in Storm's brown-and-white fur and his floppy little ears fizzed with magical power.

What was happening?

A big streak of golden glitter shot straight at Ross. It bounced off him at a sharp angle and whizzed towards Miss Armitage. Some of the glitter flowed into the small bag she was holding and then

shot back towards Kelsey. The golden
sparkles swirled around Kelsey for a few
seconds and then disappeared, just like
that, leaving her with a very suspicious
feeling.

Chapter
FIVE

'Storm? What did you just do?' Kelsey
asked in an urgent whisper. She looked
round the classroom, but everything
looked just as it always did.

'I have found a way to make sure
that Ross makes lots of friends!' Storm
woofed, looking pleased with himself.

'Well, that's really sweet,' Kelsey said
carefully. 'But how are you going to do that?'

'You will see.' Storm's eyes glinted
mysteriously. Lifting a little back leg, he
began daintily nibbling his toes.

Kelsey blinked. Storm was obviously up
to something. What could it be?

'Can everyone stop whatever they're
doing? I'm about to draw the names,' Miss
Armitage called out. Once everyone had

settled down, she shook the bag and then took out two slips of paper and unfolded them. 'This year's Apple Prince and Princess will be . . .' she said, pausing for effect, 'Ross Kirk and Kelsey Fisher!'

'Yay! Three cheers for Ross and Kelsey. Hip, hip . . .'

As everyone began cheering, Kelsey sat there in stunned silence. 'Oh no,' she whispered to Storm. 'I can't do this!' She felt herself going hot and cold at the thought of having to lead the Wassail procession.

Ross was staring across at her with his mouth open. He looked as if he wished the floor would open up and swallow him.

Storm gave Kelsey an encouraging grin that showed his sharp little teeth. 'But it is good. Everyone will want to talk to you and Ross. You can help him not to feel so shy and he will make many friends!' he yapped.

Kelsey couldn't answer Storm with the whole class looking at her. She didn't get a chance to speak to him until break. 'Storm!' she scolded, once they were by themselves. 'I don't want to be Apple Princess. You'll have to use your magic to make Miss Armitage choose someone else!'

The tiny puppy's ears drooped. 'I am afraid I cannot do that. The decision has already been announced.'

Kelsey sighed deeply. 'Oh, that's just great! Thanks for nothing!'

Storm tucked his tail between his legs and rolled his big dewy eyes. 'You are angry with me. I will leave if you want me to,' he whimpered.

'Oh no, please don't do that!' Kelsey

burst out hurriedly. She had been so
concerned about how she felt that she'd
forgotten about Storm's feelings. She
pretended to bend down and fiddle with
her shoe so that she could stroke him.

'I'm sorry. I'm not really cross. I never
want you to leave!' she declared. It was
true, she thought. Storm hadn't been her
friend for long, but she couldn't imagine
life without him now.

Storm perked up again. Wagging his tail,
he wriggled his body and licked her hand.

Kelsey smiled. 'I'll just have to put up
with being the Apple Princess, won't I?
It might not be so bad if I have you with
me.' She fought down the sinking feeling
in her tummy.

'I will help you!' Storm yapped eagerly.

'Thanks. But ask me first next time,

OK?' Kelsey said.

Storm nodded and raised one front
paw. 'That means, I promise!'

Kelsey smiled at his cheeky little face.
'Let's go and find Ross and give him his
book back.'

When Kelsey handed the book to
Ross, he just gaped at her.

'It's all mended. How did . . .'

'I'm just naturally brilliant at fixing things!' she joked. *At least, Storm is*, she thought, imagining Ross's face if he knew the truth. 'So no one's getting double detention!'

Kelsey and Storm had just turned into her street after school the following day. She saw the car parked outside her house and remembered that Jo and the twins were coming round.

As she walked into the front garden, the house door opened and Anna and Louise came bouncing out. 'Hiya, Kelsey!' they chorused.

'Hi,' Kelsey greeted them.

'Me and Louise were going to take Storm for a walk before you got back from school,' Anna said.

'We looked everywhere for him, even in your bedroom, but we can't find him,' Louise put in. 'Your dad reckons he might have run away again.'

Kelsey felt a stir of frustration. It didn't seem to occur to the twins that she might not like them poking around in her room.

'Storm's . . . er . . . got a secret hiding place he goes to when I'm at school,' Kelsey stammered. 'You two stay here. I'll go and find him.'

She went upstairs and changed out of her school clothes and then came back down to the sitting room with Storm trotting beside her.

'There he is!' shrieked Louise, kneeling down and making a big fuss of Storm.

'Where were you hiding, you naughty boy?' Anna scolded. She rolled Storm on

to his back and tickled his pale tummy.

Storm gave a small yelp of surprise. 'Be careful with him. He's only tiny,' Kelsey said sharply.

The twins looked at her in surprise. 'Sorry, Storm,' Anna said in a subdued voice, being more gentle.

'You did not need to worry, Kelsey. Anna and Louise were not hurting me,' Storm woofed, when the twins moved away.

Kelsey nodded. 'I know that really. I didn't mean to snap. It's just that I can't get used to having the twins round here all the time. I liked it when it was just Dad and me,' she whispered.

Her dad came into the room. He'd just been to order a takeaway pizza. 'It'll be at least half an hour. They're quite busy,' he said.

'There's just time for Louise and me to take Storm for a walk, then. Can we, Kelsey?' Anna asked.

Kelsey sighed inwardly. Once the twins got an idea in their heads they never let up. She still didn't like the idea of letting

Storm out of her sight. What excuse
could she give now for refusing to let
anyone else take him for a walk?

Jo came in and put some more logs into
the wood-burning stove. 'Congratulations,
by the way!' she said to Kelsey, with a
broad grin. 'It's quite an honour to be the
Apple Princess and lead the procession.'

'Um . . . yes, I know,' Kelsey said, her
tummy tightening with nerves, but she
smiled back. She was warming to Jo more
and more as time passed, especially after Jo
had taken her side about keeping Storm.

'How much does it cost to speak to
you now, Your Majesty?' Louise chimed
up, doing a silly curtsy.

Anna made sweeping up and down
movements with her arms towards Kelsey.
'We are not worthy!' she mocked.

Despite herself, Kelsey grinned. 'Silence, peasants!' she ordered in a posh voice, going out of the room, with Storm at her heels.

'That's told you two!' Jo said, laughing at the twins' stunned faces. 'Good for you, Kelsey!'

Chapter
SIX

Kelsey was just coming out of the bathroom
when the phone rang early the following
morning. 'I'll get it, Dad!' she called,
running downstairs. Storm ran down after
her. 'Hello?' she spoke into the phone.

'Er . . . Hi. It's me,' said a nervous voice.

'Ross?' Kelsey said, looking at Storm.

There was an awkward silence on the
other end of the phone. 'I . . . um . . . wanted

to ask you about this . . . er . . . Wassail
thing in the orchard. You must know all
about it. You've lived in Long Morton for
ages, haven't you?' Ross asked hesitantly.

'Yeah, I was born here,' Kelsey said.
'Wassail nights in the old apple orchard
are brilliant fun. It's noisy and exciting
and there's yummy food. We always have
a great time. But I've never been Apple

Princess before. I'm going to be dead nervous,' she admitted.

'You are?' Ross said, sounding surprised. 'I thought it was only me.'

'No way!' Kelsey said. 'Who wouldn't be worried about having half the town watching them parading about in a cloak and crown?'

'Yeah, I guess so,' Ross agreed. 'My dad's not very happy about the Wassail ceremony, either. He thinks I'll be making a real fool of myself in front of everybody.'

Kelsey suddenly began to realize why Ross might be so quiet all the time.

'Well, for a start, there'll be morris dancers on Wassail night too and my uncle Billy is one of them. I'd like to hear anyone tell him he looks a fool! He has to duck his head when he walks into our house and he's about as wide as a wardrobe.'

'I'll tell Dad that! He'll be quite
relieved.' Ross started laughing.

He had a nice laugh and Kelsey
joined in. 'I have to go now,' she said
apologetically. 'I need to take Storm for a
quick walk before school.'

'You've got a dog?' Ross asked with
new interest. 'I love dogs.'

'Yes. Storm's my new puppy,' Kelsey
told him. 'He's absolutely gorgeous. I
usually take him to the park. Hey, you live
near there, don't you? I could call for you,
if you like.'

'Yeah? That would be brilliant!' Ross
exclaimed.

'I'll be right there!' Kelsey said goodbye
and then hung up. She bent down to
bury her face in Storm's soft fur. 'I think

your magic is working already!'

Kelsey and Storm passed a neighbour's house on their way to Ross's. Kelsey noticed that there was a new poster in the window. It read, PUPPY WALKERS NEEDED URGENTLY. PLEASE RING FOR DETAILS. And there was a phone number.

She pointed the poster out to Storm. 'I wonder what that's about.'

Storm gave a doggy shrug as they walked on.

A few minutes later, Kelsey and Storm stood on Ross's doorstep as the front door opened and Ross appeared.

'Hi!' she said brightly. 'This is Storm.'

Storm woofed a greeting and wagged his tail eagerly.

'Hello, boy! Aren't you cute?' Ross said as he bent down to stroke the tiny puppy. He glanced up at Kelsey. 'He's a little King Charles spaniel, isn't he?'

Kelsey was surprised that Ross could tell which breed Storm was. 'You seem to know a lot about dogs,' she said.

Ross smiled. 'I'm always reading dog books and watching programmes about them on TV.'

'Me too. Dogs are the best,' Kelsey said.

As they wandered down the front
garden, a stern voice called out, 'Ross?
Wait there a moment, please.'

Kelsey looked round to see a man with
shiny swept-back hair. Ross's dad wore a

coat over a smart suit and he was holding a laptop bag. 'Hello there, young lady. You must be Kelsey Fisher from Ross's class.'

Kelsey nodded. 'Hello, Mr Kirk,' she said politely. 'We're taking my puppy, Storm, for a walk before school.'

'So I see.' Mr Kirk eyed Storm, but he didn't speak to him or bend down to stroke him as most people did. He looked at Ross. 'Just don't try to talk me into having a dog. I won't have one of the unruly messy creatures in the house. You know the rules.'

Ross thrust his hands into his pockets. 'Worst luck,' he mumbled, so that only Kelsey heard him. 'See you after work, Dad,' he said more loudly.

His dad nodded curtly. 'Mind you're not long. I don't want you being late for school.' He walked past them and began striding down the street.

Kelsey rolled her eyes at Storm. Ross's dad seemed very strict.

'What is unruly?' Storm woofed quizzically.

Kelsey bent down to pat him. 'It means badly behaved,' she whispered.

Storm drew himself up and his bright blue eyes flashed. 'I am not unruly!' he woofed indignantly.

'Of course you're not,' Kelsey soothed. 'I think you're just perfect!'

'What are you saying to Storm?' Ross asked.

'Oh, just stuff about going walkies!' Kelsey said hastily. 'Dogs love that.'

Storm barked and danced about, wagging his tail.

Ross smiled as they crossed the road and went into the small park. He produced an empty crisp packet from his pocket and scrunched it into a ball for Storm. Kelsey watched as Ross threw it and Storm raced about, floppy ears and swishy tail flying out behind him.

'That's it, boy. Fetch!' Ross cried happily, throwing the crisp packet again.

Kelsey smiled at Ross's face, which was glowing with pleasure; he looked as if he had completely forgotten about being shy.

Chapter SEVEN

The following day, Kelsey was in class, gluing shiny beads on her crown. Some of the other kids were making drums or putting dried beans into painted tins for musical instruments. She could see Ross concentrating hard as he painted gold squiggles on his crown.

Storm was curled up under Kelsey's desk, watching as she wiped her hands clean. Kelsey heard him give a little bark of welcome. She turned to see Jo walking into the classroom carrying a box and a big roll of bendy willow.

Jo came over to say hello to Kelsey. She had come to show Kelsey's class how to make willow lanterns. 'I make woven willow baskets and garden ornaments for a hobby,' she explained.

'Oh, very smart!' Jo nodded towards Kelsey's crown as she arranged her stuff on a nearby empty desk. 'You'll be a splendid Apple Princess, wearing that.'

'Thanks,' Kelsey said. She had worked really hard and was proud of how well it had turned out.

'I like Jo,' Storm woofed.

'Me too,' Kelsey whispered back, surprised at herself. She really meant it.

Making willow lanterns turned out to
be great fun. Jo showed everyone how
to bend and tie the soaked twigs into
shape. Even Ross seemed to be enjoying
himself making an oval-shaped lantern
that looked like a spaceship.

'Don't forget to make a little door so
you can reach in and light the lantern,' Jo
instructed.

Kelsey made triangle shapes, which she was going to join up into a star shape. When one of her willow triangles plopped on to the floor, Storm sprang to his feet in surprise and ran out from under the desk. Growling softly, he bounced down on to his front paws and then grabbed the willow triangle in his mouth and tossed it about.

Luckily, everyone else was too busy to notice. Kelsey had to try really hard not to burst into laughter as Storm went skidding across the room with the triangle, almost falling over his soft front paws.

At the end of the session, Jo gathered up all her equipment. She came to say goodbye to Kelsey. 'I could come round early on Saturday. Would you like me to help you get ready? I'm pretty good with sparkly hairspray and silver make-up.'

Kelsey nodded. 'Yes, please.'

'OK, then. See you later.'

Kelsey waved to Jo as she left. She was starting to think that being the Apple Princess might not be so bad after all.

'Oh, yuck!' Kelsey said, as Storm rolled in something particularly smelly in the grass. It was Friday night and she had decided

to take Storm for a quick run in the park
on their way home from school.

Storm stood up and shook himself.
His whole body rippled and then the
movement reached his tail, which twirled
about happily.

He looked so pleased with himself
that Kelsey burst out laughing. She
was carrying a cardboard box with her
finished crown inside. Placing it on the
grass, she bent down to scratch the tiny
puppy under his chin where the fur was
still clean.

'You mucky pup!' she said fondly.
'Phew! You'll have to go straight into the
bath when we get back!'

Kelsey picked up her box again and
tucked it under her arm. As she and
Storm started walking towards the park

gates, Kelsey spotted a familiar figure
sitting on a nearby bench. It was Ross.

Kelsey and Storm went over to him.
'Hi,' she said. 'What are you doing here?'

'Oh, hi.' Ross looked up in surprise.
'Just . . . um . . . thinking about tomorrow
night. You know, having to lead the
Wassail ceremony,' he said nervously. 'I
come here when I want to have a think
about things. It'd be great if I had any
brothers or sisters to chat to, but it's just
me and Dad.'

'Humph! What's so great about
brothers and sisters? My dad's girlfriend's
got twins. Anna and Louise are always
trying to get me to do stuff with them
and messing about and teasing me.'

'I wouldn't mind that. That sounds like
fun to me,' Ross said. 'And you'll never be

lonely with those two around.'

Kelsey blinked at him in surprise. She'd never looked at it like that before.

Ross's face changed. 'Are you bringing Storm with you tomorrow night?'

Kelsey nodded. She was planning to make him a neck-ruff later from sparkly wrapping paper. Storm would look very smart as she walked along in her royal robes, holding him in her arms.

'Could . . . could I . . .' Ross began.

'What?' Kelsey said.

'I was going to ask you if I could hold Storm for a little while tomorrow night. I wouldn't feel so scared if he was with me. But I'll understand if you say no . . .' Ross said hesitantly.

'Er . . . yeah!' Kelsey said after a second's hesitation. 'Of course you can.' She swallowed her disappointment. 'As long as Storm doesn't mind.'

As Kelsey bent down to stroke him, Storm looked up at her with wide blue eyes and nodded. 'It is kind of you to put Ross's feelings before your own,' he yapped.

'That's settled, then,' Kelsey whispered. She stood up again. 'You can hold Storm while we're leading the procession.'

'Thanks.' A wistful smile touched Ross's lips. 'You're so lucky. You've got a really close bond with Storm, haven't you? I'm hoping for a puppy for my birthday next week, but Dad's dead set against it.'

After Ross had left for home, Kelsey and Storm wandered back through the park. Kelsey's soft heart went out to the lonely boy. 'Ross would be great with a puppy, but he hasn't got much chance of ever getting one of his own, has he? Unless . . . Storm! I've just had a brilliant idea!' she exclaimed.

Storm listened intently. When she had finished he nodded eagerly. 'It is a very good plan!'

Kelsey felt a familiar tingling down her spine as Storm's brown-and-white fur

glowed with sparks. A shimmery golden mist appeared in the air. In the centre of it, a poster formed with writing on it. PUPPY WALKERS NEEDED URGENTLY. PLEASE RING FOR DETAILS.

Storm huffed out a stream of golden sparkles. The poster swirled into the air on the cloud of his breath and zoomed away invisibly towards Ross's house.

'I just hope Mr Kirk gets the message when that plops through the letterbox!' Kelsey said.

Storm nodded. 'Me too!'

Chapter
EIGHT

Back home, Kelsey put the cardboard box, with her crown safely inside it, down beside the sofa and then went into her dad's office with Storm trotting along beside her.

'Hello, love. How was school?' her dad said, looking up from his computer.

'Not bad,' Kelsey replied. 'I was going to make some hot chocolate. Do you want some?'

'No thanks,' he said, switching his computer off. 'Goodness me, look at the time! I'd better start cooking supper. Jo and the twins will be here soon.'

Kelsey found that she didn't mind this unexpected announcement quite as much as she usually would have. Talking to Ross about the twins had made her think a bit differently about them. She followed her dad into the kitchen. 'What are we having?'

'Spag bol,' her dad said, looking in cupboards. 'At least, we were,' he groaned. 'I seem to have run out of tinned tomatoes and spaghetti!'

'Da-ad!' Kelsey said, grinning and shaking her head. 'Never mind. Me and Storm will pop back out to the corner shop and get some.'

'Would you? Thanks, love,' he said, fishing money out of his trousers' pocket. 'Then I can at least make a start.'

Kelsey and Storm went to the shop. She paid for the items and they were just returning past a back entry, lined with a row of garages. One of them was open and she heard a fierce snarling and growling from inside it.

Storm whimpered and crouched down with his tail between his legs.

Kelsey swept him into her arms. He was trembling all over and she could feel his heart pattering against her hands. 'What's wrong?' she gasped.

'Shadow must be close. He has used his magic to set those dogs on to me,' he whined.

The growling got louder and Kelsey saw two dogs with pale eyes and extra-long teeth peering out of the garage. They'd see Storm at any second!

She started running down the street. There was a bus shelter across the road. It was the old-fashioned kind, with closed sides and an entrance front and back. Panting, Kelsey hurtled towards it, dashed inside and stood there clutching Storm to her.

Seconds later, she heard the fierce

dogs running past. She peeped round the shelter, but they had disappeared round the corner.

Kelsey gave a huge sigh of relief. 'It's OK. You're safe now,' she soothed. 'Those horrible dogs have gone.' Now that the danger was over, she felt weak at the knees.

Storm gradually stopped trembling, but his eyes were still troubled. 'Thank you for saving me, Kelsey. But Shadow will use his magic to make other dogs attack me. If he finds me, I may have to leave quickly without saying goodbye.'

Kelsey felt a sharp pang. She wasn't ready to lose her little friend. 'Maybe Shadow will go on past and never find you. Then you can stay here with me for good.'

Storm twisted round to look up at her,

his little heart-shaped face serious. 'That
cannot happen. One day I must return
to lead the Moon–claw pack. Do you
understand that, Kelsey?'

Kelsey nodded, but she didn't want to think about it. Maybe if she didn't mention it again, Storm would just stay forever. 'Dad's waiting for this shopping. Let's hurry back,' she said, changing the subject.

She put Storm down and he scampered along beside her. He seemed to be back to his normal self, despite his nasty scare.

Back in the house, the smell of frying onions greeted Kelsey, making her mouth water. Storm turned his head towards the sound of music and voices from the sitting room. 'Someone is here.'

'It must be Anna and Louise,' Kelsey guessed. She quickly gave her dad the shopping and then went into the sitting room. The twins were practising a dance routine to their favourite boy-band track.

They looked up and saw her. 'Hi, Kelsey.

Come and join in!' Anna invited.

'In a minute. I've just got to give these to Dad,' Kelsey said.

Louise was doing a complicated twirl. Anna pranced towards her and gave her a playful shove. Louise giggled as she lost her balance and staggered about.

'Watch out for the b–' Kelsey cried, as Louise went to sit down and missed the sofa.

But it was too late. Louise plonked down right on top of the cardboard box. There was an ominous crunching sound as it collapsed.

'My crown!' Kelsey gasped.

'Oops!' Louise's hands flew to her mouth as she stood up.

Kelsey opened the squashed box and looked inside in dismay. Her crown was in pieces. 'Oh no! Look what you've done!'

'We didn't mean it!' Anna said.

'You never do! You poke into my stuff without asking me and you're always trying to tell me what to do!' Kelsey fumed. 'Why don't you just leave me and Dad alone?' She knew that she was being unfair, but she couldn't help it. Tears sprang to her eyes. She grabbed the box with the ruined crown inside and fled upstairs.

In her bedroom, Kelsey dumped the box on her bed and threw herself down next to it, sobbing angrily.

'Kelsey?' A tiny paw reached out and patted her cheek gently. She turned her head to see Storm peering at her, his little face creased with concern. 'I will mend the crown,' he offered.

As Kelsey sat up, she felt a familiar tingling

sensation down her spine. Big golden
sparkles ignited in Storm's brown-and-
white fur and his tail bristled with magical
power. A big fountain of shimmering gold
glitter shot towards the crumpled box.

Crackle! The box straightened up and
jumped to attention. *Bang!* The top flew

open and the bits of the crown leapt out
on to the floor. *Swish!* The bits jostled
about, busily swapping places until they
fitted together like a jigsaw puzzle. But
beads and bit of decoration still littered
the bedroom floor.

There was a bright golden flash, which
made Kelsey blink hard. When her sight
cleared, she saw that the crown was
complete. It glistened and glimmered all
over like a pair of sparkling fairy wings.

'Wow! It's even better than before!
Thanks, Storm,' Kelsey gasped delightedly,
drying her eyes.

Storm gave her a doggy grin. 'You are
welcome.'

There was a tap on the bedroom door.
'Are you OK?' asked Anna.

'Can we come in?' Louise added.

'Not right now!' Kelsey said hastily.
There was no way she could explain how
the crown was sitting there in all its glory,
miraculously undamaged. 'I want to be by
myself. I'm going to glue the crown back
together and then I'll come down.'

'That's OK. We understand,' the twins
chorused in a subdued tone.

'We don't mean to boss you about and
stuff. We just go over the top sometimes,'
Anna said.

'I know. And I'm sorry I lost my
temper. I didn't mean it about leaving me
and Dad alone,' Kelsey admitted.

There was silence for a moment and
Kelsey thought the twins had tiptoed
away.

She heard whispers and then Louise
said, 'We wondered if you might like two

handmaidens on Wassail night. We could hold your cloak and stuff, if you like.'

Kelsey raised her eyebrows at Storm. She knew that this was the twins' way of saying sorry. 'OK, thanks. That sounds great,' she said, grinning.

Chapter
NINE

Saturday morning dawned crisp and clear.
'Perfect weather for Wassail night!' Mr
Fisher announced to Kelsey and Storm
over breakfast. Storm looked spick and
span and smelled of peach shower gel
after the bath Kelsey had given him,
although he hadn't been too keen on
being bathed at the time.

There was a knock at the front door.

Kelsey's dad opened it to admit Jo and the
twins.

Kelsey's spirits sank when she saw that
Louise and Anna were wearing their
riding gear.

'Oh no,' she groaned softly. Beckoning
to Storm, she quickly zoomed into the back
garden. 'They're going to invite me to go
riding with them again. I just know it!'

Storm looked up from kicking up his
heels in the frosty grass. 'Is that a bad
thing?'

Kelsey nodded miserably. 'Horses scare
me stiff and if the twins find out I'm
a scaredy-cat, they'll never stop going
on about it. I'll just hide out here until
they've gone.'

'I might be able to use my magic to
stop you being afraid of horses. Shall I
try?' Storm woofed helpfully.

Kelsey shook her head. 'Thanks, but no
thanks. I don't actually *want* riding lessons.
I'm never going to be mad about horses
like Anna and Louise . . .' She paused as

the truth of what she was saying began to sink in. She looked into Storm's calm midnight-blue eyes and she knew what she had to do.

Kelsey went back into the kitchen with Storm in her arms. Jo was sitting at the table and her dad was making coffee and toast.

'I love Saturday mornings at the stables and having riding lessons. Ponies rule!' Anna was saying.

'Are you coming with us this time, Kelsey?' Louise asked.

'Um . . . No thanks,' Kelsey said. Her heart was pounding, but cuddling Storm's warm little body gave her courage. She took a deep breath. 'Actually, horses make me very nervous. I don't really want to learn how to ride.'

Louise looked sharply at her for a moment and then she shrugged. 'OK.'

'No problem,' said Anna. 'We'll go riding with Mum and then come back here, so we can all get ready for Wassail night together. It'll be fun.'

Kelsey nodded dumbly, too amazed to speak.

'Sounds good to me,' Jo agreed. 'All sorted.'

Kelsey's dad smiled as he poured the coffee.

Kelsey felt a huge wave of relief run through her. She couldn't believe how easy that had been. She glanced down at Storm, whose big blue eyes were twinkling.

It was a clear evening and silver stars twinkled in the January sky. Kelsey's breath fogged in the frosty air as she and Storm, her dad, Jo and the twins all made their way to the old apple orchard. Kelsey wore her shining crown and cloak over her warm clothes and Storm trotted proudly beside her, wearing his smart new ruff.

Grown-ups and kids, wearing bright costumes, were already gathering in the

orchard. Delicious smells of roast apples, hot spiced cider and apple juice, and barbecued food filled the air. In one corner, a group of men were keeping watch over a crackling bonfire.

The orchard was a patchwork of gold light and deep shadows. Kelsey saw Ross waiting for her by the old gate with his dad. He wore his crown and cloak. As Kelsey and Storm went over to him, Mr Kirk smiled warmly at her, looking relaxed in jeans and a sweater.

'You'll never guess what!' Ross said to Kelsey, the moment she reached him. 'I'm going to be a puppy walker. It's a really important job. Dad fixed it up for me. Isn't that amazing?'

Kelsey beamed at him. 'It's fantastic. I'm really happy for you.'

Storm wagged his tail. 'Congratulations, Ross!' he barked, which obviously only Kelsey understood.

Ross laughed. 'It sounds like Storm's pleased for me too.' He turned back to Kelsey. 'Maybe you could help me with the puppy walking sometimes, if you're not too busy with Storm,' he said shyly.

'I'd love to,' Kelsey said.

'The ceremony's about to start,' said Kelsey's dad at her shoulder. 'They're calling for the Apple Prince and Princess.' Anna and Louise appeared and took hold of Kelsey's cloak.

Kelsey handed Storm over to Ross. Ross's eyes softened as he stroked the tiny puppy's fluffy fur. He gave Storm a cuddle and then squared his shoulders as he handed him back. 'Thanks, Kelsey, but it's only right for you to hold him.'

Kelsey nodded, smiling. Ross had a
new confident look on his face. He was
going to be all right. 'Here we go,' she
whispered to Storm as she and Ross took
their places at the head of the procession.

'This is exciting!' Storm panted eagerly.

As they moved through the trees people
beat drums, shook rattles and banged
on pots and pans. The gleaming willow

lanterns seemed to float and dance along. Everyone began singing to wake the trees from their winter sleep. 'Old Apple Tree, we'll wassail thee . . .'

It was a dramatic moment when everyone stood clear and muskets were fired through the bare branches. *Bang! Bang!* Smoke drifted upwards into the cold air.

Afterwards, Kelsey was lifted up into a tree to place cider-soaked toast on the branches. Ross had to pour cider down the tree trunk and then their part in the ceremony was over. Then everyone joined in the festivities.

'This is brilliant! It's just like a carnival!' Ross said, munching a burger.

'Told you it was fun!' Kelsey sang out as she went off to get some food to share with Storm. She waved to Anna and Louise,

who were taking part in a circle dance.

Just then, Storm gave a whimper of terror and took off through the trees.

'Storm?' Kelsey noticed sinister dark shapes with pale eyes and extra-long teeth moving through the trees.

Storm was in terrible danger.

Kelsey hurtled after the tiny puppy, stripping off her crown and cloak as she ran. She glimpsed Storm disappearing behind a wooden hut at the back of the orchard. She pelted towards it and had just rounded the building, when there was a dazzling flash of bright golden light and a fountain of sparks.

Storm stood there, a tiny puppy no longer, but a majestic young silver-grey wolf with glowing midnight-blue eyes and a thick neck-ruff glittering with a million tiny gold lights. There was an adult wolf beside him, with a wise gentle face.

Kelsey knew that Storm was going to leave. She didn't want to lose her friend, but she forced herself to be brave. If Ross could be, then so could she.

'Go, Storm! Save yourself!' she said, her voice breaking.

Storm's midnight-blue eyes softened.

'You have been a good friend, Kelsey. Farewell and be of good heart.'

'Goodbye, Storm. I'll never forget you,' Kelsey whispered as tears ran down her face.

There was a final flash of gold light and a silent explosion of sparks that drifted around Kelsey and sputtered harmlessly to the frosty grass. She heard a frustrated growl behind her as the fierce dogs slunk away.

Kelsey's heart ached, but she was glad that Storm was safe. One day her magic puppy would be the brave leader of the Moon-claw pack. 'Take care. Wherever you are,' she whispered.

As Kelsey walked back through the trees, she saw Ross coming towards her. His face was glowing with happiness and pride.

'Kelsey! I've been looking for you. I can't stop thinking about becoming a puppy walker. It's for dogs that are going to be trained as . . .'

Despite her sadness, Kelsey felt herself smiling. 'Tell me all about it. And don't miss anything out!'

Out Now

Coming Soon

Sparkling Skates   Sunshine Shimmers

APRIL 2008

puffin.co.uk

OUT NOW

A **purrfect** recipe for fun!

puffin.co.uk

Magic Puppy

A New Beginning
9780141323503

Muddy Paws
9780141323510

Cloud Capers
9780141323527

Star of the Show
9780141323534

Party Dreams
9780141323794

A Forest Charm
9780141323800

Twirling Tails
9780141323817

School of Mischief
9780141323824

Snowy Wishes
9780141323831

Classroom Princess
9780141324791

Friendship Forever
9780141324784

Sparkling Skates
9780141324777

Sunshine Shimmers
9780141324760

A little puppy
a sprinkling of magic,
a forever friend

puffin.co.uk

If you like
Magic Puppy,
you'll love

Magic Kitten

A Summer Spell
9780141320144

Classroom Chaos
9780141320151

Star Dreams
9700141520168

Double Trouble
9780141320175

Moonlight Mischief
9780141321530

A Circus Wish
9780141321547

Sparkling Steps
9780141321554

A Glittering Gallop
9780141321561

Seaside Mystery
9780141321981

Firelight Friends
9780141321998

A Shimmering Splash
9780141322001

A Puzzle of Paws
9780141322018

A Christmas Surprise
9780141323237

Picture Perfect
9780141323480

A Splash of Forever
9780141323497

Win a Magic Puppy goody bag!

The evil wolf Shadow has ripped out part of Storm's
letter from his mother and hidden the words so that magic puppy
Storm can't find them.

Storm needs your help!

Two words have been hidden in secret bones in *Classroom Princess*.
Find the hidden words and put them
together to complete the message from Storm's mother.
Send it in to us and each month we will put every correct message
in a draw and pick out one lucky winner, who will receive
a Magic Puppy gift – definitely worth barking about!

Send the hidden message, your name and address on a postcard to:
Magic Puppy Competition
Puffin Books
80 Strand
London WC2R 0RL
Good luck!

puffin.co.uk